MEG at SEA

for Hannah

MEG at SEA

by Helen Nicoll
and Jan Pieńkowski

PUFFIN BOOKS

Meg, Mog and Owl

went to
the seaside

They went out in a boat

but there was no wind

Meg made a spell

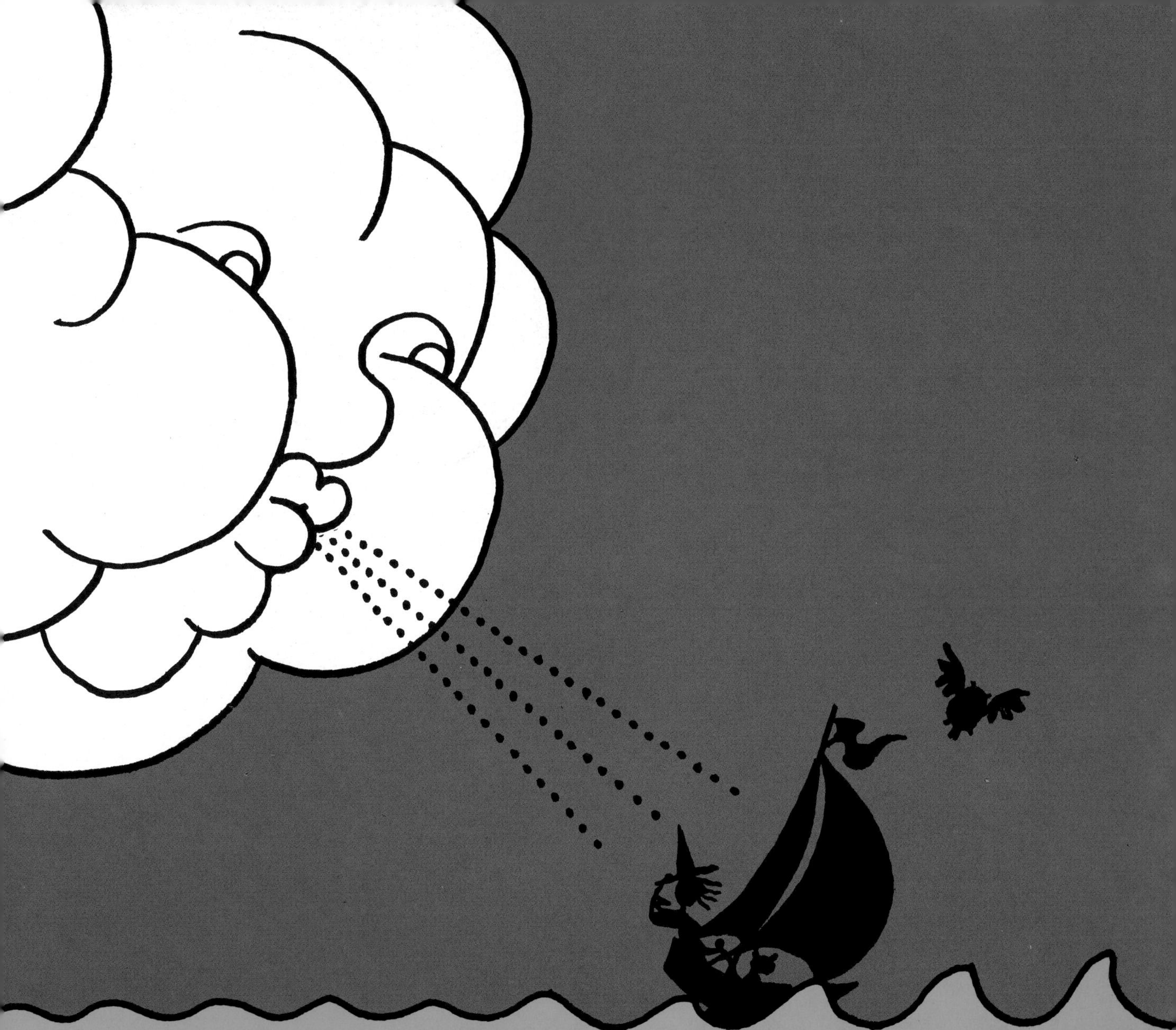

The wind blew

A storm blew up

There's land
I feel sick

The boat filled with water

and they swam to land

It
was
an
island

They were cold,

wet and hungry

Meg used a magnifying glass
to make fire

Mog and Owl
went
fishing

Mog caught a fish

Owl caught an octopus

They took the fish to Meg

EEEK
A present for you

Mog cooked the fish

Meg and Owl had a rest

Mog was lookout

He saw a helicopter

This is the code
For an awkward spot
3 dots 3 dashes
Dot dot dot
S.O.S.

Meg
made
smoke
signals
with
her
cloak

HELP
HELP

The helicopter saw them

and took them back home

Goodbye!